THE
Donkey
that
Sneezed

Val Biro

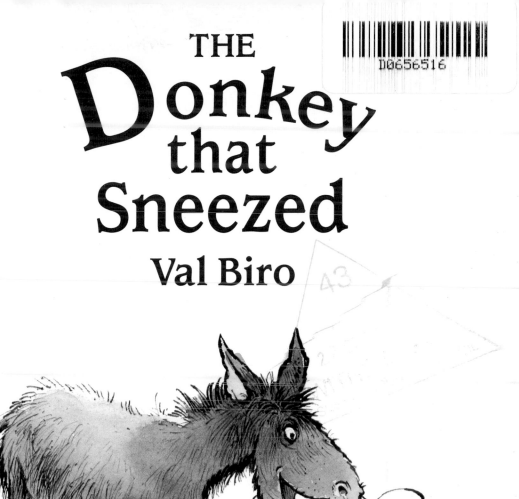

Oxford University Press

Oxford University Press, Walton Street, Oxford OX2 6DP

Oxford New York
Athens Auckland Bangkok Bombay
Calcutta Cape Town Dar es Salaam Delhi
Florence Hong Kong Istanbul Karachi
Kuala Lumpur Madras Madrid Melbourne
Mexico City Nairobi Paris Singapore
Taipei Tokyo Toronto

and associated companies in
Berlin Ibadan

Oxford is a trade mark of Oxford University Press

Copyright © Val Biro 1986
First published 1986
Reprinted 1988, 1990
First published in paperback 1990
Reprinted 1990
This edition first published 1994
Reprinted 1995
Reissued with new cover 1996

A CIP catalogue record for this book is available
from the British Library

ISBN 0 19 272308 1

Typeset by Oxford Publishing Services
Printed in Hong Kong

Once upon a time there was an old man. He had three sons: Tom, Dick and Harry.

They ate so much that soon
there was no food left in the house.

'Go out and earn your own
bread,' said the old man.

So Tom set out to seek his
fortune.

He worked for a kind old woman
who lived in a cottage.

Tom worked for a year and a day,
and as a reward the old
woman gave him a table.

She said, 'When you are hungry,
just say, "Ready, Table, Ready" –
and there will be as much food
as you want.'

So Tom took the table and went
to stay at an Inn for the night.

He was hungry, so he said,
'Ready, Table, Ready.'

At once the table was laden with food
and Tom had a good dinner.

The crooked Innkeeper had seen this
and that night he changed the
table for an ordinary one.

Next day Tom got home and said,
'This table can give us food.'
But there was no food, because
this was just an ordinary table.

The old man was angry. The
brothers were angry too, and they
beat Tom for playing such a trick.

So now it was Dick's turn to set out and he went to the same cottage.

He worked for a year and a day, and the kind old woman gave him a donkey as a reward.

She said, 'When you need money,
just say, "Sneeze, Donkey, Sneeze"
– and you will have as much
as you want.'

So Dick led the donkey away
and stayed at the same Inn
for the night.

The Innkeeper wanted his money first,
so Dick said, 'Sneeze, Donkey, Sneeze.'

The donkey sneezed, and, sure enough,
there was the money! The Innkeeper
was amazed.

That night he changed the sneezing
donkey for an ordinary one.

Next day Dick got home
and said, 'This donkey can sneeze money.'
But there was no money, because
this was just an ordinary donkey.

The old man was very angry. So
were the brothers, and now they
beat Dick for playing a trick.

This time Harry set out
to seek his fortune.

He worked at the selfsame cottage
for a year and a day. As a reward,
the kind old woman gave
him a stick in a sack.

She said, 'Just say, "Jump,
Stick, Jump" – and the stick
will jump out and beat
anyone you like.'

So Harry took the sack to
the Inn. He knew all about
that crooked Innkeeper.

When he saw the Innkeeper, Harry said, 'Jump, Stick, Jump.'

The stick jumped out and beat
the Innkeeper – Biff-baff-bump!

'Mercy! Mercy!' he cried.
'You can have all that I stole,
just stop that stick!'

So Harry stopped the stick,
took the table and the donkey
from the Innkeeper and went home.

He said, 'Ready, Table, Ready.'
And they all had a good dinner.

Then he said, 'Sneeze, Donkey, Sneeze.' And they all had plenty of money.

But he did not say, 'Jump, Stick, Jump' – because there were no crooks around.